The best mum

by Sarah Nash
illustrated by Pamela Venus

Tamarind

Tamarind Ltd

Sometimes people ask my mum,

"Do you work?"

"No," says Mum.

"But Mum...

"You say dressing me is like dressing an octopus."

"You say I'm as fussy as Pattie the poodle."

is like feeding an elephant."

"You say that when I need to get away...

"When you're in a hurry..."

"I'm slower than a tortoise."

"At bathtime...

"You work very hard and you are...

the BEST MUM IN THE WORLD!"

Look out for other Tamarind titles:

Let's Have Fun
Let's Go to Playgroup
Let's Go to Bed
Let's Feed the Ducks
I Don't Eat Toothpaste Anymore!
Giant Hiccups
Dave and the Tooth Fairy
ABC I can be

Published by Tamarind Ltd, 2003
PO Box 52
Northwood
Middx HA6 1UN
UK

Text © Sarah Nash
Illustrations © Pamela Venus
Edited by Simona Sideri

ISBN 1 870516 62 1

Printed in Malaysia